NORA and
Mrs. Mind-Your-Own-Business

OTHER YEARLING BOOKS YOU WILL ENJOY:

YEARLING BOOKS are designed especially to entertain and enlighten young people. Charles F. Reasoner, Professor of Elementary Education, New York University, is consultant to this series.

NORA
and
Mrs. Mind-
Your-Own-
Business

by Johanna Hurwitz

illustrated by SUSAN JESCHKE

A YEARLING BOOK

For Uri,
who grew up in an apartment house
6,000 miles away.

Published by
Dell Publishing Co., Inc.
1 Dag Hammarskjold Plaza
New York, New York 10017

Text copyright © 1977 by Johanna Hurwitz

Illustrations copyright © 1977 by Susan Jeschke

Yearling ® TM 913705, Dell Publishing Co., Inc.

ISBN: 0-440-45668-1

Reprinted by arrangement with William Morrow and Company, Inc.

Printed in the United States of America

First Yearling printing—May 1981

CW

Contents

The Day
They Wore Pajamas

Nobody had more friends than Nora. At least, that is what her father said whenever he rode in the elevator of their apartment building with her or whenever they walked together in the street. People might nod to Daddy, but to Nora, who was six years old, they always called out a cheerful greeting.

"Hello, Mrs. De Negris!" Nora would call back,

for she had learned the names of most of the 200 neighbors in her building. And most of them Nora considered to be her good friends. Nora's friends were all ages and sizes and breeds. Her smallest friend was Russell, who was three, a year younger than Nora's brother Teddy. Her shaggiest friend was a dog named Putzi, and her oldest friend was Mrs. Wurmbrand, who was almost eighty-five. Nora and Teddy liked to call her Mrs. W. for short.

All these friends helped to make life very interesting. Every day seemed a new adventure with new discoveries. Even the most ordinary day could suddenly turn into something special.

One Tuesday morning in the spring, just after Nora's sixth birthday, she woke up hearing unusual sounds coming from the street below. Because they lived on the seventh floor, they missed some street noises entirely, while others, like the garbage truck or fire sirens, made their way up through the air. This morning's sound was a new one. It was not one that Nora heard every day. Nora woke Teddy and told him to listen.

"What is it?" asked Teddy, puzzled.

"I don't know," said Nora. It seemed a good reason to wake up Mommy.

"I don't hear anything," Mommy said sleepily, but she went with the children to the window. Opening it and looking out, she saw that a hole had been drilled in the cement sidewalk in front of the apartment house.

"Let's go out and see," proposed Nora.

"Wait. I need my coffee first," said Mommy. Nothing ever happened in the morning until Mommy had her cup of coffee. "We'll go downstairs with Daddy in a little while," she said.

Soon the apartment was filled with morning sounds and smells. The alarm clock rang, and Daddy got out of bed and into the shower. Coffee began perking on the stove while Mommy dressed herself.

Daddy drank orange juice and coffee and ate two slices of toast, but Nora and Teddy were too excited to eat.

They put on their winter coats, toggle coats with hoods. Teddy had a brown one, and Nora had a red one. And they put on their shoes. Smart Nora tied all the laces. They were waiting at the door when Mommy and Daddy came. Daddy smelled of shaving lotion, and he carried a briefcase.

"Hurry, hurry," said Teddy. "Or they'll be all finished."

"Even if they finish drilling, they'll have to do something with the hole," promised Mommy.

As usual, when they were in a rush, the elevator took them up before they went down. But at last they reached street level.

Nora and Teddy pushed ahead. There, directly in front of their building, was a hole. As they stood looking about they could see four other holes already dug and men beginning to make a fifth nearby.

"It's the trees!" Mommy cried out with delight. "These are holes for the trees."

Over a year ago there had been a campaign along the street to collect money to plant trees. And now at last it looked as if there would really be some results.

"Good-bye," Daddy said, laughing as he kissed everyone. "I'll look for you all in the forest when I come home. Nora, you can be Little Red Riding Hood."

"Will wolves come with the trees?" asked Teddy. He looked excited, not scared.

13

"Of course not. Daddy is just joking," said Mommy.

The drillers moved on, and the number of holes on the street continued to increase. Before the morning was over, Nora counted twenty-two holes. There were eleven on each side of the street. Mommy wanted to go upstairs and make the beds, but Nora and Teddy refused to leave the excitement. Luckily it was a beautiful morning, and that, plus the drilling, drew all the neighbors out of their apartments.

Mrs. Wurmbrand came out of their building and into the sunshine. Every day when the weather was fine she went out for a walk.

"How lovely it will be to have the trees at last," she said to Mommy. "I'll watch them grow, like your children."

Next door to Mrs. W. lived another woman, whom Nora had once nicknamed Mrs. Mind-Your-Own-Business. Only she never did.

"What is this mess?" grumbled Mrs. Mind-Your-Own-Business, when she came out of the building. "If you want trees, move to the country." She never seemed happy, and today was no exception. She was the only one who was annoyed by the activity on the street. Everyone else was very pleased.

Mommy met and spoke with people she hadn't seen all winter, even though they lived only a few yards down the street. Mrs. Dworsky came pushing a carriage with her new baby, a girl named Elizabeth.

There was more excitement when another truck arrived with the trees. The trees looked small and sad, just branches without any leaves. But even big trees didn't have leaves in March, Mommy reminded Nora. The roots were wrapped up in cloth, and Nora found it hard to believe that they would ever really grow. But when the first tree was lowered into a hole, everyone applauded. The hole was filled in with earth, and the workmen moved on to the next hole.

"Nora, we really must get you washed up. It will be time for school before you know it, and you'll need some lunch," said Mommy, looking at her wristwatch.

Nora went to an afternoon kindergarten class, which she usually loved. But now she said, "I want to stay home today with Teddy and watch the trees."

"Don't be silly," said Mommy. "Teddy won't

stay here all day either." Then suddenly, looking about her, she asked, "Where is Teddy?"

He wasn't standing in the cluster of people near the planted tree, nor was he standing near the next empty hole.

"Teddy! Teddy!" called Mommy.

He was not in view at all. "Perhaps he went into the lobby," said Mommy hopefully. But she came back in a minute without him. Henry, the doorman, had not seen him since they all went out together in the morning.

Mrs. Michaels came out of the building, pushing Russell in his stroller. She offered to look about for Teddy. Perhaps he was on the next block.

"He wouldn't cross the street alone," said Mommy. She started to look into the lobby of the building next door. Even the workmen stopped their work and began to look about.

"You should call the police," said Mrs. Mind-Your-Own-Business, who had just returned from buying some groceries.

"No, no. He'll turn up in a minute," said someone else.

"I bet he went to the playground," suggested one of the workmen.

"You should keep a closer eye on your children," scolded Mrs. Mind-Your-Own Business. "A good mother wouldn't let them out of her sight."

"My mother *is* a good mother!" shouted Nora angrily.

Mommy didn't hear what was being said. She was too busy looking about for Teddy to listen to the people talking.

Nora tugged at her mother's coat. "I'll find Teddy," she said.

"No! Stay right here with me," said Mommy. "I have enough to worry about without you disappearing too." Her face had a scared look on it that Nora had never seen before.

And so it was not Nora, or Mommy, or Mrs. Mind-Your-Own-Business, or any of the workmen who found Teddy. It was little Russell. While his mother looked in doorways and up and down the street, Russell looked at what would interest a little boy. He looked at holes, and at the foot of their block, deep in a hole meant for a tree, Teddy was quietly playing in the dirt.

His coat was muddy. He had taken it off. And his clothes were muddy too.

When Mommy saw him, she didn't scold about

the dirt or about his being lost. She only said, "Teddy, why are you wearing your pajamas?" It was true. In the morning they had left the house so quickly that the children hadn't gotten dressed.

"I'm wearing pajamas too!" cried Nora, opening her red coat.

Everybody except Mrs. Mind-Your-Own-Business laughed.

The men returned to tree planting. The trees went into the holes. Mrs. Michaels and Russell went grocery shopping, and Nora and Teddy went into the house with Mommy. They put on real clothing and ate some lunch.

While they were eating, Nora said, "I don't like that Mrs. Mind-Your-Own-Business. She's mean. I bet she doesn't have any friends."

"Maybe she doesn't want to be mean," said Mommy. "Perhaps she never learned how to make friends. Some people never do."

After lunch Nora went to school where she told everyone that her brother Teddy had gotten lost in the forest where she lived.

They didn't believe her at all, but it was almost true.

Treats and Tricks

On Tuesday of the last week in October, Nora came home from school full of excitement. Everyone had been talking about Halloween. Last year Mommy and Daddy had not permitted the children to go trick-or-treating, but this year Nora was determined to convince her parents that she and Teddy should go. After all, Nora was in the first grade now and old enough to do new things.

First, however, the problem of costumes for their school parties had to be settled. The choice was easy for Teddy.

"I want to be Superman," he said.

"What do you need?" asked Mommy.

Teddy showed her the picture on the cover of a comic book that he had been given by the barber when he had his last haircut.

"Nora has some old red shorts that will do and some old navy tights," thought Mommy aloud. "All right, Teddy. All I'll have to do is make you a cape."

"Look, up in the sky," shouted Teddy. "It's a bird, it's a plane, it's Teddy Superman!"

"What about you, Nora?" asked Mommy. "What will you be?"

Nora thought. Last year she had worn an old skirt of Mommy's and lipstick and had been a princess at the kindergarten costume party. This year she wasn't sure what she wanted to wear.

"How about being a princess again?" suggested Mommy.

"That's a good idea," Teddy agreed.

But Nora wasn't satisfied. "No," she said. "This year I shall be a queen."

"Is your class going to have a party?" asked Mommy. "Will you wear your costume to school?"

"No," answered Nora. This was the moment she had been waiting for and fearing at the same time. "I'll wear my costume when I go trick-or-treating."

"Nora!" exclaimed Mommy. "You know Daddy and I don't approve of that. You children cannot go!"

"Why?" asked Teddy.

"Everyone else goes," said Nora, pouting. "All the children in my class go: Sharon, Lisa, David, Mark . . . everyone."

"No," said Mommy patiently.

"Give me one good reason," demanded Nora impatiently.

"Daddy and I decided we would rather not have you ringing doorbells and asking for candy. So the subject is closed," said Mommy. But it wasn't.

At dinner that evening, as the whole family was sitting around the table, Daddy asked his usual question about what had happened during the day. Teddy told about the new game he had played in his nursery school. Nora was silent.

Then Teddy told the story that the teacher had told his class on the flannel board. Still Nora was silent. Teddy told how Roger's mother had brought cupcakes for the whole class because it was Roger's birthday. And still Nora was silent.

"Didn't anything special happen in your class, Nora?" Daddy asked.

"Everyone talked about going trick-or-treating. Except me. Everyone in first grade is going. Why can't I go this year?" asked Nora. She was trying hard not to cry.

"Nora, you know that Mommy and I don't believe in that nonsense," explained Daddy.

"Didn't you go when you were a little boy?" asked Teddy.

"No," said Daddy. "My parents didn't let me go either. It's an old pagan custom. It isn't nice to bother people and beg for candy. I'll bring some candy home with me after I leave my office on Halloween."

"It's not the same," cried Nora. "Daddy, didn't you ever want to go trick-or-treating?"

"Yes. But I understand now what my parents meant. And someday you and Teddy will understand too," answered Daddy. "Be happy that you don't have to beg."

"We just want to show off our costumes," said Nora. "We don't want to beg."

Then Mommy spoke. "Maybe," she said, "if they just went to a couple of neighbors, like the Michaels and the Wurmbrands, to show them how funny they look in their Halloween outfits. . . ."

"Yes, yes," begged the children.

And then Nora got an idea! Suppose instead of demanding a treat from the neighbors, they brought treats and gave them away. "We could bake cookies," she said enthusiastically. "And then we could give them to people." The plan was under way.

After school the next two afternoons, the children helped Mommy bake cookies. They made two types: chocolate chip and peanut butter. Halloween was on Friday, and Mommy let Nora invite her friend Sharon to sleep over, so she could go trick-or-treating with them.

Teddy looked like a very small Superman. He almost looked as if he could fly with the red cape. But his mother made him promise to use the elevator and the stairs. "And don't try jumping down three steps at one time, Superman," said Mommy. "I don't want any broken teeth or bones."

"Superman can't break anything on himself," insisted Teddy. But he agreed to be careful.

Sharon was dressed as a gray kitten. She had a mask with little ears and a long tail.

Nora was a queen. She was wearing lipstick, eye shadow, earrings, and a long skirt. She looked very grown up. On her head was a cardboard crown covered with aluminum foil. It wasn't gold, but it did look just like silver.

"Remember, you are not begging. You are giving," said Mommy, as the trio set out holding bags of cookies.

They went up to the eighth floor and rang Mrs. Wurmbrand's bell. In a few moments the door opened. Both Mrs. W. and her daughter greeted the children.

"Trick or treat!" shouted the children.

"Just a moment. We have some chocolate for you," said their neighbors.

"No! No!" explained Nora. "We will give *you* a trick *or* a treat."

"A treat for us?" asked Mrs. Wurmbrand. "This is a new holiday that I don't remember."

Nora gave Mrs. Wurmbrand and her elderly daughter some cookies from her bag. The women kissed each of them; even Superman got a kiss. Mrs. W. also gave them each a chocolate bar.

"It's a trade," she explained, when they tried to say no.

"I didn't try too hard," Teddy admitted later.

Next door to the Wurmbrands lived Mrs. Mind-Your-Own-Business.

"Let's ring this bell," suggested Sharon.

"Maybe some cookies will cheer her up," said Nora. So they rang the bell and waited. There was no answer, so they rang again, and then again.

"I guess she isn't home," said Nora, giving an extra long push on the bell.

Suddenly the door opened, and in front of them stood Mrs. Mind-Your-Own-Business. She looked even fiercer than usual.

"Trick or treat?" shouted the children.

"I've had enough of your tricks, ringing my bell and annoying me. If you don't go away this minute, I'll call the police."

"The police!" said Teddy, his eyes opening wide. "We just wanted to give you some cookies that we made. There are two kinds."

"I don't eat cookies," said Mrs. Mind-Your-Own-Business. "My doctor doesn't allow it."

"Then we can show you a trick," said Nora.

Instantly she was on the floor and standing on her head. It was her only trick, but she was very proud of it. The long skirt fell down and covered her face, and her crown slid off her head onto the floor of the hallway, but Nora remained upside down.

"What are you doing?" demanded Mrs. Mind-Your-Own-Business.

"This is our trick," explained Teddy. "You didn't want our treat so we're giving you a trick. Do you like it? Nora's been practicing all week."

Nora was still upside down. The old woman lifted the skirt covering Nora's face.

"Can you breathe? Are you all right?" she asked.

Nora's face was as red as the lipstick she was wearing. From upside down she called, "Do you like my trick?"

"Stop! Stop this instant!" commanded their neighbor. She helped Nora right herself. "You had better have a drink of water." She invited the children inside her apartment. Instead of water she gave them each a small drink of ginger ale.

Then she began to laugh. "Do you know what? I used to be able to stand on my head once too."

Incredulously the children stared at her.

"Do you want to try it now?" asked Nora. "I could help you."

"Oh, no," said Mrs. Mind-Your-Own-Business. "I'm glad to be able to stand on my two legs these days."

The children said good-bye and went off to visit a few other neighbors: at the Michaels', little Russell Michaels greeted them at the door in pajamas that looked like a tiger skin. They stopped at several doors, for they had many good friends in the building.

When the cookies were all given away, they returned to their own apartment. They described their adventures to Mommy and Daddy.

"We even rang Mrs. Mind-Your-Own-Business's bell," Nora reported.

"Oh, Nora!" moaned Mommy. "You shouldn't have bothered her."

"It's OK," said Teddy.

"Yes," said Nora. "She didn't want any cookies, but we made her smile. I didn't even know she could."

Mommy smiled. "Too bad we forgot to save

some cookies to eat as a treat for ourselves," she said.

"That's all right," said Nora. "We got lots of candy." The cookie bags were empty of cookies but filled with other things.

"We said no begging," said Daddy, growing annoyed.

"We didn't beg," explained Nora. "We just traded."

"Well," said Daddy, taking a Tootsie Roll out of Nora's bag and putting it into his mouth. "That was a clever trick you played on me."

But he didn't seem angry.

7E—XYZ

Sometimes, after school, Nora went to play at her friend Sharon's house. One afternoon, when she came back home again, Nora said, "I wish I had my own room."

"You have a very nice room," said Mommy.

"It's not mine alone! Sharon has a room all for herself. Her bed and her toys and her books and her clothes are all separate. I want a room just for me, without Teddy."

"Our apartment has five rooms," said Mommy. "A living room, a dining room, a kitchen, and two bedrooms. Daddy and I share one bedroom, and Teddy and you share the other."

"I want *privacy*," said Nora, pouting.

The apartment could not grow bigger, and so everything remained the same. Some days Nora played happily with Teddy, and some days they had fights. And whenever they fought, Nora would say, "I want privacy. I want my own room."

Then Anita, who lived down the hall, had her apartment painted, and Mr. Emery, the landlord, installed a new refrigerator in her kitchen. In front of the building stood the empty appliance box. It was very large. Nora and Teddy and Mommy all saw it when they were walking home from Nora's school on Friday afternoon.

"That box is as big as a house," said Teddy, marveling.

"If you mean a doghouse," said Mommy.

"It's as big as a room!" shouted Nora. "Could I have it for my room?"

"What do you mean?" asked Mommy.

"Let's take the box inside, and I'll make my private room in it."

"Yes! Yes!" shouted Teddy, jumping up and down.

"But *you* can't go in it," said Nora. "It's going to be my private room."

"If that box comes into our apartment, you must let Teddy play in it too," warned Mommy. "Otherwise, out it will go!"

"He can come in when I invite him," promised Nora.

So they all pushed together and somehow managed to get the big box up the front steps of the building. Henry, the doorman, saw them coming and held the door open.

"That box has been going in and out of this building all day," he grumbled good-naturedly. "What are you going to do with it? Fill it with cookies?"

"It's a new room for our apartment," said Nora, as they pushed the box into the elevator. The box almost filled the entire elevator car. Nora and Teddy and Mommy squeezed themselves in close to the walls, and Teddy pushed the button marked 7.

Their apartment was 7E.

"This box will be called 7N—*N* for Nora," explained Nora proudly.

"It will be *N* for Nobody, unless you let Teddy in too," reminded Mommy. Her voice was a little bit angry. "I don't want to regret letting you bring this box into the house," she warned.

"Let's call it 7E—XYZ," said Nora, compromising.

The children's bedroom was a good size. So there was enough space in one corner, if they pushed the toy box aside, to fit the box into the room.

Mommy brought a knife from the kitchen and cut a door in the cardboard.

"Make a window too," instructed Nora.

"Please," said Mommy. She made two windows.

"OK, it's ready to play in," said Mommy. "Remember, no fighting. I've got to start cooking supper." She left the children and went off to the kitchen.

"Teddy, you can play with my new clay," said Nora, as soon as Mommy was out of the room.

Delighted, Teddy sat down at the little table and

began to play with what until then had been forbidden to him.

Nora took out her poster paints. Very carefully, so as not to drip any paint, she opened the little jar of black paint. She painted a doorknob.

Then she painted 7E—XYZ in the center of the door. She wanted to paint the entire box red or blue to make it look pretty, but she knew it would take too long. Besides, she had only very small jars of paint. So instead, she painted a picture of herself on one side of the box (the side that Mommy wouldn't notice when she walked into the room), and under it she painted her name in block letters: NORA.

When Daddy came home, he admired the new apartment within their apartment. Nora wanted to eat supper in the box, but Mommy said no.

"Please," begged Nora.

"Absolutely not!" said Mommy. "And that's final."

So Nora joined the family at the table in the dining room.

Mommy and Daddy were expecting company that evening. Some of their friends were coming to have coffee and to visit. After their baths, Nora

and Teddy were permitted to remain up to say hello to the guests. Teddy kept running into the living room and taking peanuts from the bowl that Mommy had filled. But Nora was having too much fun in apartment 7E—XYZ to come out. She put her blanket and pillow inside.

Around eight thirty the doorbell rang. Nora reluctantly left her apartment to greet the guests, even though she usually liked to stay up and meet the company. Then it was bedtime. Both Nora and Teddy tried to postpone the moment.

"Can't we stay up longer?" begged Nora. "There's no school tomorrow."

"I'm hungry," said Teddy. He said that every night at bedtime.

"Here," said Daddy, grabbing two apples from the fruit bowl. "You can take these to your room and eat them."

"Nora, you're in charge of turning off the light," said Mommy. She kissed both children good-night.

Teddy sat on his bed, eating his apple.

Nora took her apple into apartment 7E—XYZ. It was cozy eating inside the box.

"Can I come in?" asked Teddy.

"*N-o* spells no," said Nora with authority.

"Please."

"No!"

"I'll tell Mommy," threatened Teddy, using his only weapon.

"You can come in tomorrow. Tonight I need my privacy," said Nora from inside the box.

Teddy looked through the little window. "Are you going to sleep in there?" he asked.

"Yes!" Nora answered quickly. She didn't tell Teddy that he had just given her the idea.

The children threw their apple cores into the wastebasket. Nora's missed, and she had to pick it up off the rug and aim for the basket more carefully. She wiped her sticky fingers on her pajamas, and then she turned out the light.

"Good night, Teddy," she said, as she crawled into the privacy of her little apartment.

"What is it like in there? Is it dark?" asked Teddy.

"Dark," agreed Nora.

"Is it scary?"

"No, silly," said Nora. "It's just dark and private."

"Aren't you lonely?"

"No," Nora assured him.

"I'm lonely for you to be in your bed," complained Teddy.

"You know I'm right here," said Nora.

"I want to see you."

There was a moment of silence. Then Nora said, "OK, you can come into my house for a minute."

"Can I bring Jason?" asked Teddy. Jason was his favorite teddy bear, and it was in bed with him.

"OK," said Nora, "but you can't bring any others." Teddy slept with a whole army of bears in his bed.

Teddy got out of bed, and by the faint light that came under the closed door he made his way to the doorway of 7E—XYZ.

He cuddled up next to Nora.

She giggled. "Isn't this fun?"

They pressed together in the dark, whispering.

The light coming through the bedroom window woke Nora in the morning. The first thing her eyes focused on was the big cardboard box across the room.

Mommy, coming into the bedroom, said, "Do

you remember falling asleep in the box last night? Daddy had to put you and Teddy into your beds."

Nora couldn't remember that at all.

"I'm glad you agreed to let Teddy inside apartment 7E—XYZ," said Mommy.

"I guess Teddy can share my privacy with me," explained Nora.

The Night
They Slept in Clothes

It was five o'clock in the afternoon. Nora was sitting on the bedroom floor playing with her dollhouse, Teddy was in the bathroom washing paint off his hands, and Mommy was in the kitchen cooking dinner. Daddy would be home soon. Suddenly the light flickered overhead, and then it went out.

"Mommy," Nora called. "The bulb burned out."

"Mommy," Teddy called. "I can't see anything."

Mommy came from the kitchen.

"We must have blown a fuse," she explained to the children. "The kitchen light is out too. All the lights seem to be out," she said, turning on the light switches about the apartment to test them. "It's lucky that there's still a little light outside so we can see to find the fuses."

Nora ran to the window and looked out. "Mommy," she called. "Come here! Everyone is looking out the window."

Teddy and Mommy came running. Sure enough, from almost every window in the buildings across the street heads were poking out. It was an unusual sight and looked very funny.

Mommy raised the window, and the cold air came into the room.

"Do you have lights?" called a voice from across the street.

"No!" shouted Mommy. "There must be a power failure."

"What's a power failure?" Nora asked, as her mother closed the window.

"There is something wrong with the electricity. Something is broken."

"How could it break?" asked Teddy.

"Shhh, I'll explain later," said Mommy. "I have to find the candles now."

Already it was very dark in the apartment. They could hardly see anything. But Mommy felt about in the kitchen cupboard and found a box with some candles in it. Soon two candles were burning in the kitchen and gave a small light.

"Now we're set till the power is fixed," Mommy said, looking about.

Teddy didn't say anything. In the dim candle-light he looked scared.

"Teddy," Mommy said, laughing, "what a lucky night this is. We're going to have an old-fashioned night."

"What's that?" asked Teddy.

"Well, first of all, we're going to have supper by candlelight. In the olden days that was the only light there was."

"I want more light," said Teddy.

"I'll light more candles," said Mommy. "It's going to be lots of fun. And Daddy will be here very soon."

She looked at the kitchen clock. In the dim light it still said five o'clock.

"Look," said Mommy. "The hands on the clock aren't moving. They won't be able to move until the electricity is fixed."

"Mommy, come here," called Nora. She was back at the window. The street was as black as night. Even blacker.

"The streetlamps must be broken too," observed Nora.

"They use the same electric power that we do," explained Mommy.

In the windows across the street they could see burning candles and people waving flashlights.

"This is fun," cried Nora.

Mommy went back to the kitchen, and Teddy followed.

"Light more candles now," he insisted. Mommy lit two more.

They heard a noise at the door and then the sound of banging. Mommy went toward the door. "Who is it?" she called.

"It's me. Open the door. I can't find the key-hole."

It was Daddy's voice, so Mommy opened the door. Daddy was out of breath. "I had to walk up,"

he explained, "since the elevator isn't running."

The hall was perfectly dark without lights.

"It's just a miracle that I was riding home on the bus and not the subway. There seems to be a big power failure along the west side of the city."

Suddenly Nora realized something. "If Daddy is home already, it means that I missed my TV program," she complained.

"No TV this evening," said Daddy. "Without electricity there is no television, no radio, no refrigerator, no dishwasher, no—"

"What about the telephone?" asked Mommy. "I must phone my parents. They may be worried."

"And you ought to call Mrs. Wurmbrand," said Daddy. "Even though her daughter is with her now, she may be nervous. Check that they're OK and that they have candles. The phone has its own cables and shouldn't be affected by the power failure."

"I can't get a dial tone," Mommy called from the phone.

"Give me a flashlight, and I'll go upstairs to the Wurmbrands," said Daddy. "Want to come along, Teddy?"

"No," said Teddy. "I want to stay here."

"Ask them to come and have supper with us," said Mommy. "They could even sleep here if they want. Perhaps you ought to check on Mrs. Ellsworth too. She's all alone." Mrs. Ellsworth was the real name of Mrs. Mind-Your-Own-Business.

Daddy took the flashlight from Mommy and put a few candles in his pocket before he left the apartment.

Supper was ready to be served when Daddy returned alone. "The Wurmbrands and Mrs. Ellsworth took the candles and thanked you for the invitation. But they are all afraid of walking down the stairs in such a dim light. They're going to stay together in Mrs. W.'s apartment until the power is restored," he informed everyone.

The family sat down around the kitchen table. It was very cozy with the candlelight shining on the plates. There were hamburgers and baked potatoes. Mommy had put little birthday candles in the potatoes.

"Can we make a wish even if it isn't our birthday?" asked Nora.

"Of course," said Mommy.

"I know what I'm wishing for," said Daddy. "Light!"

"I'm wishing that you'll wash the dishes, since the dishwasher isn't working," said Mommy.

"You're not supposed to tell wishes," said Nora.

"That's right," said Daddy. "But I got the hint, so I guess Mommy's wish will come true, anyhow."

The birthday candles were blown out, and the eating began.

"Broccoli tastes better in the dark," observed Teddy.

"I'll have to remember that," mused Mommy.

"We can't have baths tonight," announced Nora.

"Why not?" asked Daddy. "The water is still working."

"Because it's too dark to see if we're dirty, and it's too dark to see if we get clean."

"Will you read to us while Daddy washes the dishes?" asked Teddy.

"Yes. I mean no," said Mommy. "It's too dark. We'll have to skip bedtime stories tonight. Just straight off to bed. No stories, no baths."

"No pajamas," Teddy whined. "I don't want to put on my pajamas, and I don't want to go to sleep in the dark."

"You always sleep in the dark," said Nora. "And when you close your eyes, it's dark."

"But when I open them it's light again, and it's never dark like this. I don't like the dark," said Teddy.

"I have an idea," said Mommy. "Since this is such a crazy day without electricity, let's make it a crazy night too. You and Nora can go to bed with your clothes on if you want to. But you must take your shoes off," she added quickly.

Both Teddy and Nora loved the idea. "Let's go to bed right away," shouted Nora.

Mommy turned to Daddy and winked.

She carried one of the candles to the children's bedroom. The candle was quite burned down, but it would last until they were tucked into bed.

"Good night," she said, kissing them both. She gave them their good-night hugs and hugged Teddy's favorite bear Jason too. "In the morning the lights will probably be working fine again."

"And the TV," said Nora.

The children snuggled under their covers so delighted by the strange feel of their clothing that they forgot to be alarmed by the absence of light shining in under the door.

For a while they giggled and talked together. And then, in the dark, they fell asleep. They slept

so well that they didn't notice in the middle of the night when the light suddenly went on overhead.

Daddy tiptoed into the bedroom and turned it off.

In the morning things were back to normal. Nora protested when Mommy made her change into fresh clothing before she went off to school.

"But I'm already dressed," Nora insisted.

"You're still dressed for Tuesday," explained Mommy. "And now it's Wednesday."

When they were eating breakfast, they saw that the hands on the kitchen clock showed two thirty, which was the wrong time. Before leaving for work, Daddy changed the time on the clock. Nora wondered about what happened to the time that got lost. "It was never three o'clock or four o'clock or . . ." she argued. "All the hours got lost in the dark."

"No," said Daddy. "Tuesday evening didn't get lost. You'll probably remember it longer and better than half the other days of your childhood."

Know-It-All Nora

Now that Nora was in first grade, she seemed to know many more things. In school she had already half completed the first reading workbook. She had learned to tie her own shoes, and she knew how to tell time—except for those times like twenty to eight or ten after four, which were hard to remember.

She could also color inside the lines in her coloring books, and she knew how to pump her legs on the swings in the playground. Nowadays, Nora seemed to know it all. Knowing so much was part of growing, but it wasn't until her first baby tooth fell out that Nora really felt that she was grown up.

The tooth had not even been loose.

For some time Nora had admired the wobbly teeth in the mouths of her friends. Sharon's tooth was loose for two weeks before it came out. Arthur's loose tooth came out in school when he poked at it in class. Amy's gum bled when her tooth fell out. At night in bed, Nora felt her teeth expectantly. They all seemed very secure. She bit hard into firm apples, carrot sticks, and pieces of meat. The teeth remained firm as ever.

"Why won't my teeth fall out?" Nora asked.

She was almost seven now, old enough to lose a few teeth. Some of her classmates bragged that they lost their first teeth when they were still five years old.

Mommy watched Nora examining her teeth in the mirror. "I can remember the morning when you were seven months old and woke with the first tooth beginning to show in your mouth. And now you want it to fall out," she mused.

"How long do you think I will have to wait?" asked Nora impatiently.

"I don't know," Mommy answered. "I only know you cried and cried before each tooth grew in. What a hard time it was for Daddy and me."

Nora laughed. "What did you do when I cried?"

"Sometimes we held you, and sometimes we put you in the crib and closed the door and let you cry."

"Then what happened?" asked Nora.

"In a little while your crying made me feel so sad that I would pick you up and hold you again," said Mommy.

"I'm glad," said Nora.

"Yes," said Mommy. "And I'm glad that you won't be crying when the new teeth come in."

Three weeks later, when Nora bit into her slice of raisin toast at breakfast, her tooth fell out.

"It wasn't even loose," shrieked Nora with delight.

"Let me see the tooth," begged Teddy. He was as sad as Nora was happy. It would be a long time before he lost any teeth. Nobody ever lost a tooth when he was four.

"I'm so happy today isn't Saturday," cried Nora, running back from the bathroom mirror where she had gone to admire the little space between her teeth.

"Why?" asked Daddy.

"So everyone at school can see me!" said Nora, grinning a wide, proud smile. The space was small but evident.

Mommy looked carefully into Nora's mouth. "I think I can see the new tooth already starting to grow."

When Nora went off to school, she wanted to take the little baby tooth with her.

"Leave your tooth at home and just show everyone the hole," advised Mommy. "If you lose your tooth, you can't put it under your pillow—"

"—for the tooth fairy!" shouted Teddy.

It might be the first tooth that Nora had lost, but both children knew all about the tooth fairy, who came and put money under a child's pillow in the night.

"What does the tooth fairy do with all the old teeth?" asked Nora, admiring the tiny tooth in her hand.

"Maybe he eats them," suggested Teddy.

"Maybe he is a *she,*" said Mommy.

"Maybe he is a *they,*" said Daddy.

So Nora went to school while the tooth remained in the apartment in a glass on her bookshelf. In the evening, after Nora had brushed all of her remaining teeth, the little tooth was wrapped in a tissue and put under her pillow.

Nora felt like the princess who slept with a pea under her mattress. The tiny tooth seemed like an enormous lump under her pillow, and it kept her awake long after Teddy had fallen asleep. It was Nora's plan to remain awake and to see the tooth fairy. She closed her eyes for a few moments, and then she must have fallen asleep. She was awakened by a whispered voice near her head.

"I can't find it," said the voice, which sounded like Mommy's.

"Should I turn on the light?" asked a second voice. It too was familiar. It sounded like Daddy.

"No, get a flashlight."

Nora's eyes adjusted to the darkness. She felt a movement beneath her pillow, and she recognized Mommy's laugh.

"Thank goodness," Mommy said with a sigh. "I found the tooth."

Nora sat up in bed. "Mommy," she said accusingly. "Why are you taking my tooth away? It's for the tooth fairy."

There was silence for a moment. Then Daddy said, "Nora, why aren't you asleep?"

"I'm waiting for the tooth fairy," said Nora. But already the truth was dawning upon her. "Isn't there a real fairy? Why are you looking for my tooth?"

The room was quiet. Only Teddy's deep breathing could be heard across the room. From time to time he made a little snore. Nora sniffed back some tears that she felt coming to her eyes.

"I wanted to see a real fairy," she said.

Mommy and Daddy sat on the edge of her bed, and Mommy leaned over and kissed Nora in the darkness. "Don't be sad," she whispered, so as not to wake Teddy. "Think what a big girl you are now that you're getting your permanent teeth."

"Look at it this way," said Daddy. "You can say that you are related to the tooth fairy."

Nora sniffed again and smiled. She was beginning to feel a little better. It was fun to sit talking with Mommy and Daddy in the dark.

"Nora," said Mommy. "You're such a big girl now. Can I ask you a favor? Don't tell Teddy yet.

He doesn't know this. So let's keep the tooth fairy a secret until he's a bit bigger, like you."

"Nora, you seem to know everything these days," said Daddy. "That shows that you're really growing up."

"There's one thing I still don't know," Nora whispered to her parents in the dark.

"What is that?" asked Mommy.

"I don't know how much money you put under my pillow," said Nora.

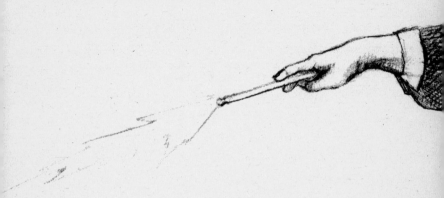

The New Baby-Sitter

". . . and so Cinderella married the handsome prince and they lived happily ever after."

Mommy closed the book as Nora and Teddy sighed with satisfaction at the ending of the story.

"I wish I had a fairy godmother," said Teddy.

"I could use one myself," said Mommy. "I need someone to turn a banana or a book into a baby-sitter."

Nora giggled at the thought of a banana becoming a baby-sitter. "Who will be our sitter?" she asked.

It was Sunday. Mommy and Daddy had concert tickets, a gift from Mr. and Mrs. Michaels, who had been invited away for the holiday weekend with little Russell. That meant, of course, that Mrs. Michaels would not be baby-sitting with the children as she usually did when their parents went out.

"Perhaps Anita is free this evening," said Mommy. She dialed their neighbor's phone number, but there was no answer. Then she dialed the number of one of the teen-age girls who had occasionally stayed with the children in the past. No luck.

"Could Grandma and Grandpa come and stay with us?" asked Nora.

"No, they both have bad colds," Mommy explained. "I spoke with them this morning."

"If you can't get a sitter," said Daddy, looking up from his crossword puzzle, "then you go alone, and I'll stay with the children."

But Mommy said no. She was determined to find a sitter for the children. She made three more phone calls. Each was unsuccessful. One sitter was busy, another had the flu, and the third was not home.

Nora had an idea. "Let's ask Mrs. Wurmbrand. She would be a wonderful sitter," she said, thinking of the chocolates their elderly neighbor usually brought with her.

Both Mommy and Daddy vetoed that suggestion, explaining that Mrs. W. was over eighty years old. "She is our friend," said Mommy, "but we can't ask too much of her. It wouldn't be fair. Her daughter has come to help take care of her now, not to take care of you. The Wurmbrands can't be asked to baby-sit."

But thinking of Mrs. Wurmbrand gave Mommy an idea. Next door to the Wurmbrands lived Mrs. Ellsworth, whom they usually referred to as Mrs. Mind-Your-Own Business. Though she was sometimes sour and unpleasant to the children, Mommy was feeling desperate. Mommy decided to go upstairs and prevail in person upon Mrs. Ellsworth to mind their business or, more specifically, Teddy and Nora during the hours of the concert. Ten minutes later Mommy returned elated. Mrs. Mind-Your-Own-Business had agreed to act as baby-sitter.

Nora was curious. What kind of baby-sitter

would she be? Mrs. Michaels was wonderful. She read to the children or played Parcheesi and Chinese checkers. Grandpa made up new stories when he came. The other sitters usually sat watching TV most of the time.

Teddy felt like crying. He did not like new baby-sitters.

Supper was over quickly, and Nora and Teddy were bathed and in pajamas when Mrs. Mind-Your-Own-Business rang the doorbell. Both Mommy and Daddy thanked her profusely as they went off.

Mrs. Ellsworth had never been in their apartment before. She looked around and ran her finger over the top of the coffee table. "Sticky!" she said half to herself, but Nora heard her.

Then she walked over to the bookshelves that lined the living-room wall. "Heavens! What a load of dust catchers all these books are. You can't possibly read them all," she fussed, rubbing her fingers along the dusty tops of the books and examining her hand.

"Mommy and Daddy read lots of books," Nora reported proudly. "I can read now too. Do you want to hear me?"

She was disappointed when Mrs. Ellsworth said no.

"Would you like to see me stand on my head again?" Nora offered, remembering her Halloween success.

"Oh, no thank you," said Mrs. Ellsworth, but she gave Nora a smile. It was her first of the evening.

"Do you want to see our room?" asked Nora, and she led the woman into the room she shared with Teddy.

Their neighbor gasped. "Heavens! How many toys you have! Do you really need so many?"

"My friend Sharon has more toys than this," reported Nora, "and she doesn't even have to share them."

"There are lots of things that I need," said Teddy. Both Nora and Mrs. Ellsworth looked at him. These were the first words that he had spoken since his parents had left.

"What can you possibly need?" asked their sitter. "You have enough toys here for a whole kindergarten!"

"I need something better than toys," explained Teddy.

"Ice cream?" asked Nora.

"Children eat too much ice cream and too much candy," said Mrs. Mind-Your-Own-Business sternly. Until that moment Nora had been hoping that she had brought some chocolate or some other treat in her pocketbook the way Mrs. W. did.

"And chewing gum!" added Mrs. Ellsworth. "It is disgusting the way young children are always chewing gum."

"Teddy doesn't get chewing gum," Nora declared. "He always swallows it."

"What I need," said Teddy, ignoring his sister, "is something very special."

"Mrs. Wurmbrand is a special friend of ours," said Nora. "She is our pretend grandmother."

"Well," said Mrs. Mind-Your-Own-Business, picking up a rag doll from the floor and examining it critically, "I guess I could be an aunt."

"We already have three aunts and seven great-aunts," said Nora. "You had better be something else, Mrs. Woolworth."

For a moment, Mrs. Ellsworth looked a little hurt. "Ellsworth," she corrected Nora. "Well, tonight I am your baby-sitter. I guess that's enough."

"What I need," said Teddy, "and what Nora

needs too," he added generously, "is a fairy god-mother."

"Yes!" shrieked Nora with delight. Sometimes Teddy had the most wonderful ideas, even though he was only four years old.

"What do you mean, a fairy godmother?" de-manded their baby-sitter.

"You know," said Nora. "It's in all the stories. Cinderella and Sleeping Beauty, they had fairy god-mothers. You give us our wishes."

"That's just nonsense," scoffed Mrs. Mind-Your-Own-Business. "Those are just make-believe stories. Besides I don't know any magic. I can't grant wishes."

"That's true." Nora sighed with disappointment. "It was such a good idea."

"A pretend fairy godmother," said Teddy, his face very serious as he spoke, "does pretend magic."

"How does that work?" asked their baby-sitter.

"First you give me a wish," instructed Teddy. "Then I tell you what I want. Try it."

"If it's candy," conceded the pretend fairy god-mother, "I have a roll of Life Savers in my pocket-book. But you must brush your teeth afterward."

Teddy shook his head. "Tell me I can have a wish."

"Teddy, I grant you one pretend wish," said the old woman solemnly.

"You need a magic wand," shouted Nora. She ran to the toy box, and after a minute of rummaging about she dug out a stick that had come with a toy drum for Teddy's last birthday.

Mrs. Mind-Your-Own-Business took the stick and waved it in the air.

"I wish I had an alligator," said Teddy.

The fairy godmother gasped at the request. "But-but-but," she sputtered. Nora walked over and whispered to her. Mrs. Ellsworth nodded and smiled.

"Teddy," she said, "I grant you a pretend alligator."

"Where is he?" asked Teddy.

Nora answered for the fairy godmother. Teddy might have invented the game, but Nora was quick to improvise and even to improve upon it. "The alligator is in the bathtub. He's invisible so no one can see him."

Teddy clapped his hands with pleasure. A pretend alligator, like a pretend fairy godmother, was better than none at all.

"Now give Nora a wish," he said.

Mrs. Mind-Your-Own-Business was prepared to grant anything. The game was very simple now that she understood how to play.

For a moment Nora was silent. Then she said, "I wish for a roll of Life Savers."

Mrs. Ellsworth had a little difficulty waving her wand and opening her pocketbook at the same time. But she managed and granted Nora's wish by giving her a roll of assorted flavors. It was a started package, not brand-new as Nora had hoped.

Teddy began to protest. "Nora should get pretend candy like my pretend alligator," he said. But Nora quickly promised to share her booty with him and gave him the first candy, even though it was her favorite color: red.

The children each sucked on one candy and brushed their teeth under the supervision of their fairy godmother.

"Now I wish you would go to sleep," said Mrs. Ellsworth.

The children each kissed their fairy godmother good-night and climbed into their beds. Mrs. Ellsworth turned out the light and closed the door. She was smiling to herself with pleasure and relief because baby-sitting and even making magic were much easier than she had ever supposed.

Inside the darkened bedroom, Teddy whispered to Nora. "Too bad we didn't get a *real* fairy godmother."

"I know," Nora whispered back. "But I know something else, Teddy. We got a new friend who *is* real, and that's even better."

And it was.

MS READ-a-thon —
a simple way to start
youngsters reading

Boys and girls between 6 and 14 can join the MS READ-a-thon and help find a cure for Multiple Sclerosis by reading books. And they get two rewards — the enjoyment of reading, and the great feeling that comes from helping others.

Parents and educators: For complete information call your local MS chapter. Or mail the coupon below.

Kids can help, too!

Mail to:
National Multiple Sclerosis Society
205 East 42nd Street
New York, N.Y. 10017

I would like more information about the MS READ-a-thon and how it can work in my area.

Name _____
(please print)

Address _____

City _____ State _____ Zip _____

Organization _____

1—80